Library of Congress Cataloging-in-Publication Data is available.

10 9 8 7 6 5 4 3 2 1

Published by Sterling Publishing Co., Inc.
387 Park Avenue South, New York, NY 10016
© 2004 by Amanda Haley
Distributed in Canada by Sterling Publishing
c/o Canadian Manda Group, One Atlantic Avenue, Suite 105
Toronto, Ontario, Canada M6K 3E7
Distributed in Great Britain and Europe by Chris Lloyd at Orca Book
Services, Stanley House, Fleets Lane, Poole BH15 3AJ, England
Distributed in Australia by Capricorn Link (Australia) Pty. Ltd.
P.O. Box 704, Windsor, NSW 2756, Australia

Printed in China

Sterling ISBN 1-4027-1708-3

I Wish Santa Would Come by Helicopter

PICTURES BY AMANDA HALEY

Sterling Publishing Co., Inc.
New York

Mommy, I wish Santa would
come by helicopter.

Then, Maxie, who would
drive his sled?

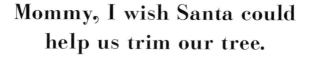

Mommy, I wish Santa could
help us trim our tree.

Then, Maxie, who would
trim Santa's tree?

Mommy, I wish Santa could
have dinner with us.

Maxie, I didn't cook enough dinner
for Santa and eight reindeer!

Mommy, I wish Santa could bring
our family a big motorboat.

But how would Santa put
a large boat in a small helicopter?

Mommy, could Santa have a sleep-over?

**Santa is so big . . .
and the extra bed is so little!**

Mommy, I wish Santa
could kiss me good-night.

Dear, Santa's beard is so tickly!

Mommy, I don't want to go to sleep.
I wish Santa could read to me.

Maxie, if he stayed here and read to you,
then who would deliver presents to your friends?

Mommy, I can't sleep. I wish I could stay up all night and be Santa's helper.

Maxie, it's cold and dark outside and delivering presents is hard work.

What if Santa came on Christmas morning
to help me open my presents?

That's a good idea. But now, my tired boy,
I have your Santa wish list.

Mommy, did Santa come by helicopter?

Merry Christmas!